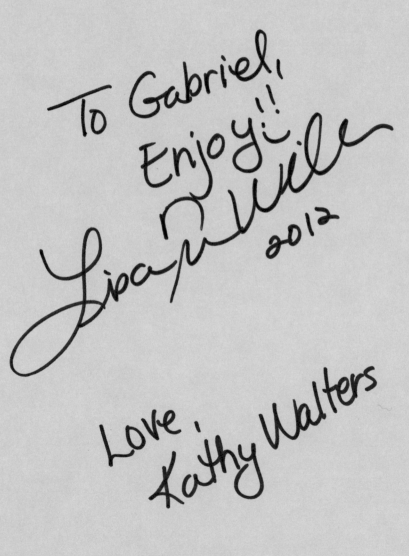

To Gabriel,
Enjoy!!
Lisa McMill
2012

Love,
Kathy Walters

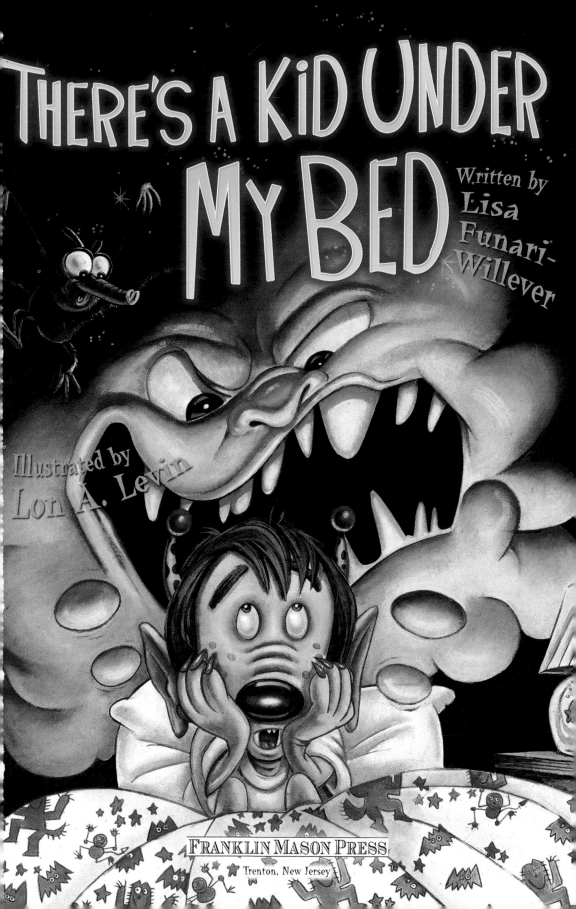

There's a Kid Under My Bed

Written by
Lisa Funari-Willever

Illustrated by
Lon A. Levin

FRANKLIN MASON PRESS
Trenton, New Jersey

The editors of Franklin Mason Press would like to thank those who work tirelessly selecting the winners of our Guest Young Author and Illustrator contest. Your care in selecting the work of young writers and artists today will help to shape and inspire the authors and illustrators of tomorrow.

Editorial Staff: Marcia Jacobs and Faustiene Smith

Cover and interior design by Peri Poloni-Gabriel,
Knockout Design, www.knockoutbooks.com

Published in the United States.
Printed in the United States of America
Franklin Mason Press
ISBN 978-0-9760469-4-3
Library of Congress Control Number: 2008924653

°Cystic
Fibrosis
Foundation
...adding tomorrows every day.

Franklin Mason Press is proud to support the important work of the Cystic Fibrosis Foundation. In that spirit, $0.25 from the sale of each book will be donated to this wonderful organization. To learn more about their work, read our About the Charity page at the end of the book or visit www.cff.org.

To my own little monsters,
Jessica, Patrick, and Timothy…LFW

I dedicate this book to Joanne,
who is the light of my life…LL

In memory of
Sharon Bortle,
mother, teacher,
friend, lover of
books and writing.

In the far off town
of Monsterville,
behind the huge oak tree,
was a little
monster cottage
and a
monster family.

Now, in this little cottage
with his father
and his mother,
lived little monster,
Marshall,
and Fred,
his older brother.

They did the things
all monsters do,
they worked
and played
and sang.
And twice a day
they flossed and brushed
in between each fang.

They went to monster
hockey games and
swallowed flying pucks.
Their favorite sport,
of course, was watching
giant monster trucks.

At monster **school,** the monsters **learned** what monsters need **to know...**

how to **read** and **write** and **roar** and even **how to sew.**

And every
monster cottage
had a little
monster broom,
and every little monster
learned to tidy up
his room.

Marshall and his brother,
fought like all young
monsters do.

Playing
tricks on
one another,
with paint
and mud
and glue.

Now, every night
in Monsterville,
beneath the setting sun,
little monsters went to sleep,
while bigger ones had fun.

Marshall was just
six years old
and Fred was
so much stronger.

But just like Fred,
Marshall wished
that he could
stay up longer.

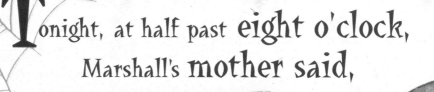

Tonight, at half past eight o'clock,
Marshall's mother said,

"Marshall, get your jammies on.
     It's time to go to bed."

"Just a little longer,"
     Marshall begged to stay up more.
"It's getting late," his Mama said.
     "Don't make your Papa roar."

"But I'm not even sleepy and
     these rules are so unfair.
Everyone is having fun
     and I'm alone upstairs."

"**A** little monster scaredy-cat,"
teased his brother, Fred.
"Maybe there's a scary kid
underneath your bed!"

"Don't scare your little brother,"
mother monster,
she declared.
"There's no such thing
as kids,
so there's no reason
to be scared."

"But Fred said kids are big
and mean and
very, very tricky.

They hide in closets,
under beds
and some are really sticky."

But Mama wasn't joking
so he hurried to his room.

And just in case
he saw a kid,
he thought he'd bring the broom.

He found some foot pajamas,
in his favorite color red,

Grabbed a monster teddy bear
and hopped into his bed.

Mama Monster
tucked him in
and kissed him on the nose.

Then told him kids
are make-believe,
from scary
late night shows.

With his little monster
night light and
his little monster broom,
Marshall lay there in the darkness,
looking all around the room.

He saw a shadow moving
and hollered,
"Mama, please!"
But Mama pointed
to the branches,
swaying on the trees.

She tucked him in one more time
and very firmly said,
"There's no such thing
as kids, you know.
They're only in your head."

He hid under the covers
        'til he heard a giant growl.
He screamed
        and Papa ran right in,
            to find a monster owl.

"Can I please sleep in your room,
just this once,
just for tonight?
I'm sure a kid will jump out
when he knows you're out of sight."

"I promise you'll be fine,"
Papa said and gave a wink.
"Wait, don't go," Marshall cried.
"I think I need a drink."

So Mama brought some water
and tucked him in
once more.

But Marshall hollered,
"Mama, wait!"
before she reached the door.

"Now, what is it?"
Mama asked,
her eyes about to glow.
"I drank too much
and now I think
I really have to go."

When Marshall crept back to his room,
he had one last request,
"Mama, can we check the bed,
the closet, and the chest?"

"I'm sure there's something in here
and I bet it wants to eat,
something soft and squishy
like a Marshall Monster treat."

Mama checked the closet twice
and then she checked the chest.
"The coast is clear," she smiled.
"Now will you get some rest?"

"I know just where that kid has hid,"
little Marshall said.
"He's where Fred said all kids hide...
underneath my bed."

"Fine," Mama Monster sighed,
kneeling on all fours, pulling up
the bedspread and looking at the floor.

Then Mama started laughing
with the loudest monster funnies.
"There's nothing here except
a dozen monster-size dust bunnies."

"It's only dumb old dust bunnies?"
he asked her in her ear.
"It seems like monster allergies
are all you have to fear."

Marshall hopped down next to Mama
and wiped his furry brow,
"I guess we're safe tonight,
because there's no kid down here now."

"Well, you better get to sleep,"
Mama handed him the broom.

"You'll need your rest
tomorrow...
when you're sweeping up
your room!"

JORDAN STRATTON
Age 8, Red Bank, NJ, Fairview Elementary School

Pig In Hot Chocolate

1st

Once there was a pig who was very valuable and it had wings. One day the pig smelled something – it smelled like mud. So he flew to the farmer's house. Then he flew in and saw a big glass of mud and he flew into the glass. The pig said, "This doesn't taste like mud, it doesn't smell like mud and it doesn't feel like mud." So the pig tried to fly out of the glass but he smacked right into a cookie. He tried to fly out from the other side but he ran into a marshmallow storm. In the sky, he saw chocolate chips so he flew up and ate all of them. He said, "That was very good." The farmer came in and said, "Who ate all of my chocolate chips?" Suddenly, he saw the pig and he brought him back to the barn.

He put him to sleep, went back to his house, and enjoyed his hot chocolate.

EZRA CAMPOS-PEREIRA
Age 7, Bloomfield, NJ, Fairview Elementary School

Lazy Bones

2nd

Once there was a boy who worked all day until midnight. Here are some of his chores. First, he would go to the fields to milk the cows. Then he would go around town to pick up the garbage. He always did a lot of chores and he had no fun at all. Until one day when a lazy person came by. Even though the person was lazy, he knew it was time to give the boy a break. So the lazy person helped him and by the next week, the boy only had two chores left. After that, he was as happy as could be.

LINDA ANN RODRIGUEZ
Age 7, Middletown, NJ, Fairview Elementary School

Wet, White, and Blue

3rd

One day there was a girl named Lin. Lin loved the snow and she especially liked to play in it. She loved to make snowmen and drink hot cocoa. She loved to color and draw the snow. She loved snow so much, she even wrote a poem about it: *There was snow that fell down, it was wet, white, and blue and it fell on the ground.* Lin thought snow was fun to see and eat. When it was hot outside she would think about snow and smile. Then she loved it even more.

Guest Young Illustrator

PETER MATTHEWS
Age 9, Kinnelon, NJ,
Stonybrook Elementary School

Cabin

KATE DOLPH
Age 8, Kinnelon, NJ,
Stonybrook Elementary School

My Yellow Lab, Luke

MICHAEL SHAMOUIL
Age 8, Verona, NJ,
F. N. Brown Elementary School

George the Painter

Would You Like To Be An Author or Illustrator?

FRANKLIN MASON PRESS is looking for stories and illustrations from children 6-9 years old to appear in our books. We are dedicated to providing children with an avenue into the world of publishing.

If you would like to be our next Guest Young Author or Guest Young Illustrator, read the information below and send us your work.

To be a Guest Young Author:

Send us a 75-200 word story about something strange, funny, or unusual. Stories may be fiction or non-fiction. Be sure to follow the rules below.

To be a Guest Young Illustrator:

Draw a picture using crayons, markers, or colored pencils. Do not write words on your picture and be sure to follow the rules below.

Prizes

1st Place Author / 1st Place Illustrator

$25.00, a framed award, a complimentary book and your work will be published in FMP's newest book.

2nd Place Author / 2nd Place Illustrator

$15.00, a framed award, a complimentary book and your work will be published in FMP's newest book.

3rd Place Author / 3rd Place Illustrator

$10.00, a framed award, a complimentary book and your work will be published in FMP's newest book.

Rules For The Contest

1. Children may enter one category only, either Author or Illustrator.

2. All stories must be typed or written very neatly.

3. All illustrations should be on 8.5" x 11" paper and must be sent in between 2 pieces of cardboard to prevent wrinkling.

4. Name, address, phone number, school, and parent's signature must be on the back of all submissions.

5. All work must be original and completed solely by the child.

6. Franklin Mason Press reserves the right to print submitted material. All work becomes property of FMP and will not be returned. Any work selected is considered a work for hire and FMP will retain all rights.

7. There is no deadline for submissions. FMP will publish children's work in every book published. All submissions are considered for the most current title.

8. All submissions should be sent to:

Youth Submissions Editor, Franklin Mason Press
P.O. Box 3808, Trenton, NJ 08629
www.franklinmasonpress.com

About the Cyctic Fibrosis Foundation

What is Cystic Fibrosis?

Cystic fibrosis (CF) is a disease you are born with that affects the lungs and the digestive system, making it hard for those with CF to breathe and to take in all the good nutrients from the foods they eat. One in ten Americans is a carrier without symptoms of the defective CF gene.

CureFinders®

CureFinders® is the Cystic Fibrosis Foundation's school-based fund-raising program for grades K-12. It is a simple change-collection program that provides students with the opportunity to raise money for a disease that affects young people just like them. It is children helping children, and the result is more money, support and awareness for cystic fibrosis.

Cystic Fibrosis Foundation
...adding tomorrows every day.

CureFinders cf

To learn more about *CureFinders®* and the Cystic Fibrosis Foundation, call **1-800-FIGHT CF** or visit us online at **www.cff.org**

The Story of 65 Roses®

The story of 65 Roses® began in 1965, when a woman by the name of Mary G. Weiss joined the Cystic Fibrosis Foundation as one of its many volunteers. Mary was a very passionate and dedicated volunteer, as her three young boys had cystic fibrosis. She wanted to do everything in her power to help find a cure.

On a typical day, Mary began her routine of calling family, friends and community members to tell them about CF and ask them for help in her and the Foundation's quest to find a cure for the disease. After several calls, Mary's 4-year-old son, Richard, who had been listening to her every word, came into the room. "I know what you're working for," said the young child, startling his mother. Richard did not yet know he had CF. "What am I working for, Richard?" she asked, to which the boy responded, "You are working for 65 Roses."

Speechless, Mary went over to him and tenderly hugged her young son. He could not see the tears streaming down her face as she said softly, "Yes, Richard, I am working for 65 Roses."

From that day forward, "65 Roses" has become what children of all ages often call their disease, since the words are much easier to say than "cystic fibrosis." But making it easier to say doesn't make the disease any easier to live with.

The "65 Roses" story has captured the hearts and emotions of all who have heard it. The rose, appropriately the ancient symbol of love, has become the symbol of the Cystic Fibrosis Foundation.

65 Roses® is a registered trademark of the Cystic Fibrosis Foundation.

About the Author and Illustrator

LISA FUNARI WILLEVER is the author of 16 books for children and teachers and is married to Todd Willever, a Captain in the Trenton Fire Department. They have three children, Jessica, Patrick, and Timothy Todd and they are adopting a little girl from Moldova. While she treasures her thirty-four years in the historic city of Trenton, NJ, she is proud to reside in beautiful Mansfield Township, NJ. A graduate of Trenton State College, she loves nothing more than traveling with her family and visiting schools all over the world.

LON LEVIN is the award-wining illustrator and the man behind the monsters. The illustrator of many renowned books, he has been the Senior Art Director for Warner Brothers Worldwide Marketing Services, helped launch the Power Rangers and X-Men and has received numerous Illustration and Design Awards. A graduate of Art Center College of Design in Pasadena, CA, he lives in Hollywood with his wife, Joanne and Golden Retriever, Sebastian.

About Franklin Mason Press

FRANKLIN MASON PRESS was founded in Trenton, New Jersey in September 1999. While our main goal is to produce quality reading materials, we also provide children with an avenue into the world of publishing. Our Guest Young Author and Illustrator Contest offers children an opportunity to submit their work and possibly become published authors and illustrators. In addition, Franklin Mason Press is proud to support children's charities with donations from book sales. Each new children's title benefits a different children's charity. For more information, please visit

www.franklinmasonpress.com

FRANKLIN MASON PRESS

PO Box 3808, Trenton, New Jersey 08629